This book belongs to:

....

To read with:

....

For Lucan, my Second Assistant – C.F.
To Valeria and Daniel – M.A.

PICTURE SQUIRRELS

First published in 2015 in Great Britain by Barrington Stoke Ltd
18 Walker Street, Edinburgh, EH3 7LP

www.picturesquirrels.co.uk

This paperback edition first pubished 2016

Title of the original German edition: "Gawain von Grauschwanz und die Schreckliche Meg"
(extract from: *Leselöwen – Rittergeschichten*) © 1994 Loewe Verlag GmbH, Bindlach

Translation © 2015 Barrington Stoke
Illustrations © 2015 Mónica Armiño

A CIP catalogue record for this book is available from the British Library upon request

ISBN 978-1-78112-527-4

Printed in China by Leo

Cornelia Funke Mónica Armiño

Gawain Greytail
and the Terrible Tab

PICTURE SQUIRRELS

Raven Castle was full of mice. The mice were very happy and content in their castle home.

But the lord of Raven Castle, Sir Tristan of Twitstream, was not very happy. His best chainmail was all chewed up. His wife was tired of shaking mouse droppings off the cheese. Their six children didn't want to play with half-nibbled dolls any more.

So Sir Tristan of Twitstream rode into town to buy a cat. The cat's name was Tab. She was scary, sleek and silent, with claws as sharp as knives. And Tab was always, always hungry. She was the best mouser in the land and Sir Tristan paid ten gold coins for her.

Back at the castle, Tab got to work. Within a month, only three mice were left – Shuffle, Snuffle and Scuffle. The three of them were nothing but skin and bones. Tab stood guard by the larder so they could not get near. And when they tried to sleep she lay down in front of their mouse hole and blew her fishy cat breath inside.

"There's nothing else for it," Shuffle said. "We need to find a new home!"

"But where?" Scuttle cried. "We are castle mice. And there are no other castles near by."

Poor Snuffle said nothing. He just chewed on the end of his whiskers.

Things were very bad.

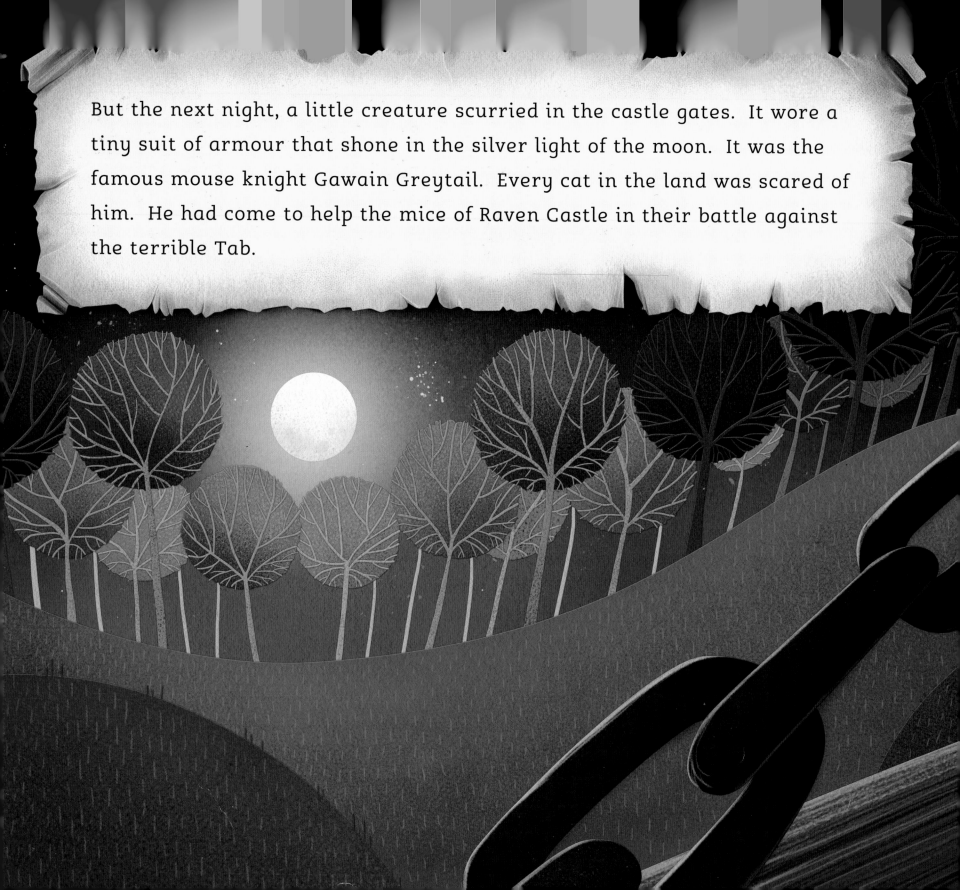

But the next night, a little creature scurried in the castle gates. It wore a tiny suit of armour that shone in the silver light of the moon. It was the famous mouse knight Gawain Greytail. Every cat in the land was scared of him. He had come to help the mice of Raven Castle in their battle against the terrible Tab.

"I have dealt with worse," Gawain said, as he twisted the ends of his mousy whiskers. "First of all, we need to get you some armour and three big sharp needles. Forks would be a good idea, too."

"I can get forks and needles," Scuttle whispered. "But where will we get armour from?"

"We will make it," Gawain said. "A few metal cups, a candle flame and ..." He pulled a tiny club from his belt. "We will hammer the hot metal into shape with this. Now let's get to work!"

The three castle mice nodded.

Three times they were interrupted by the terrible Tab and three times brave Gawain led her away. The cat didn't catch so much as the tip of his tail.

"This cat isn't so smart after all," Gawain said. "She might be fast, but ..." He twirled his mousy whiskers. "I am far faster."

The three castle mice looked up at him in wonder. Then they put on their armour. It was not as splendid as Gawain's, but it would protect them against sharp cat claws. They looked at themselves in a bit of broken mirror and giggled.

"Don't we look dangerous?" Snuffle said.

"You look like knights," Gawain said. "Real live knights. Now, take the needles and forks and we will chase Tab from Raven Castle for ever."

And so the mice tiptoed through the dark castle on silent paws.

The human castle-dwellers had gone to their beds long before. Sir Tristan's snores boomed around the Great Hall.

Terrible Tab lay in front of the glowing fire, sharpening her claws on a chair. When Gawain, Snuffle, Scuffle and Shuffle ran towards her, she jumped up in surprise.

"Helloooo!" she purred. "Yum yum. Dinner *and* pudding."

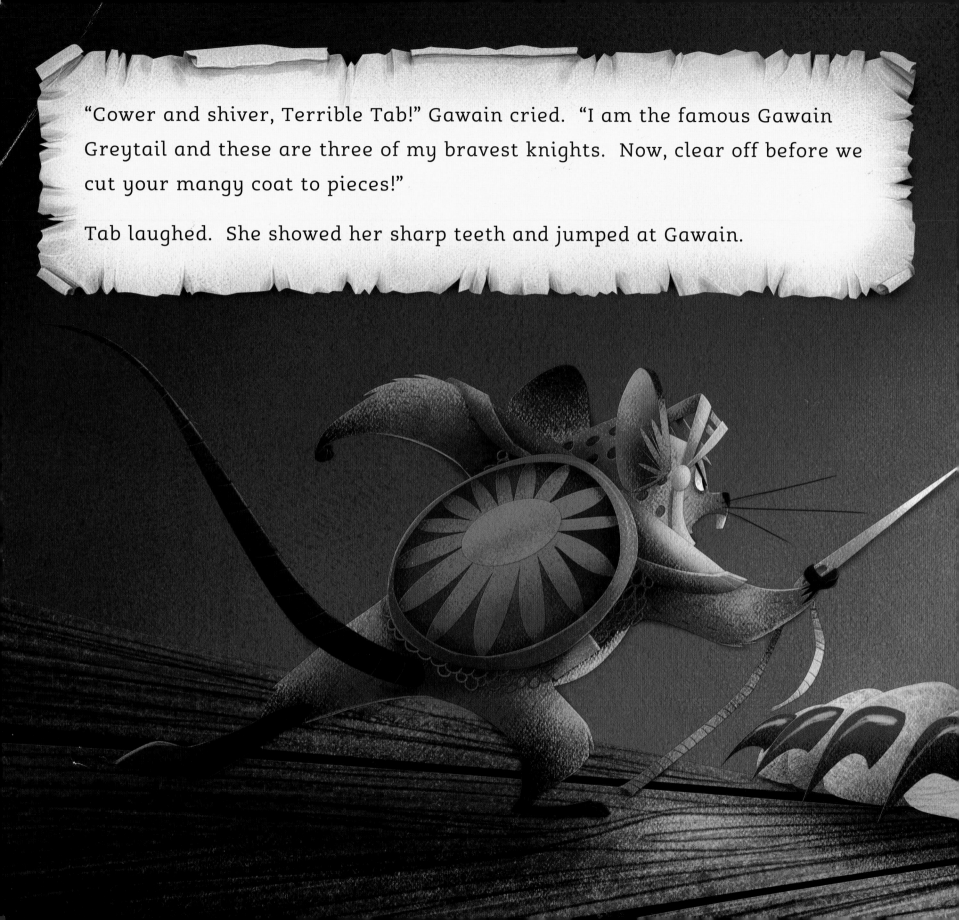

"Cower and shiver, Terrible Tab!" Gawain cried. "I am the famous Gawain Greytail and these are three of my bravest knights. Now, clear off before we cut your mangy coat to pieces!"

Tab laughed. She showed her sharp teeth and jumped at Gawain.

Gawain took a neat step to one side and Tab landed with a thump on her nose. She hissed and set her claws on the mice like daggers, but they skittered off their armour and onto the stone floor.

"Clear off, Tab!" Scuttle shouted and he poked Tab with a sharp needle.

"Yes, get lost!" Shuffle waved his fork under the cat's nose.

"We were here first!" Snuffle cried, as he chopped off one of Terrible Tab's whiskers.

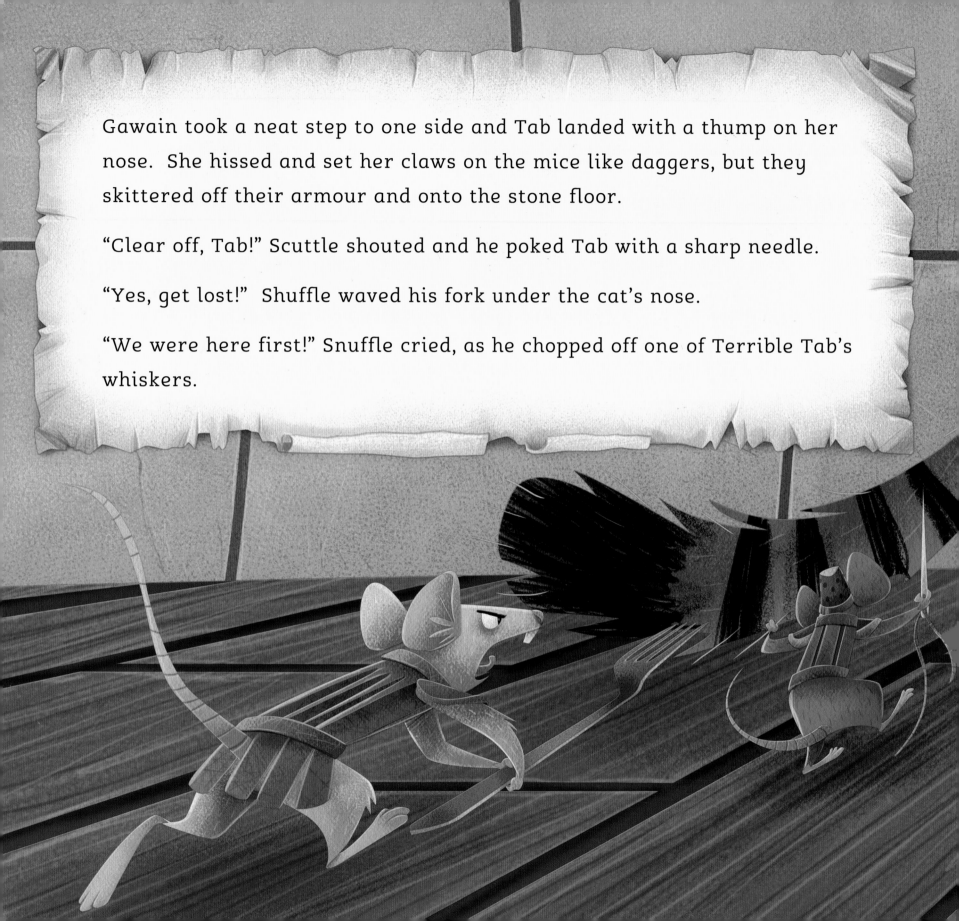

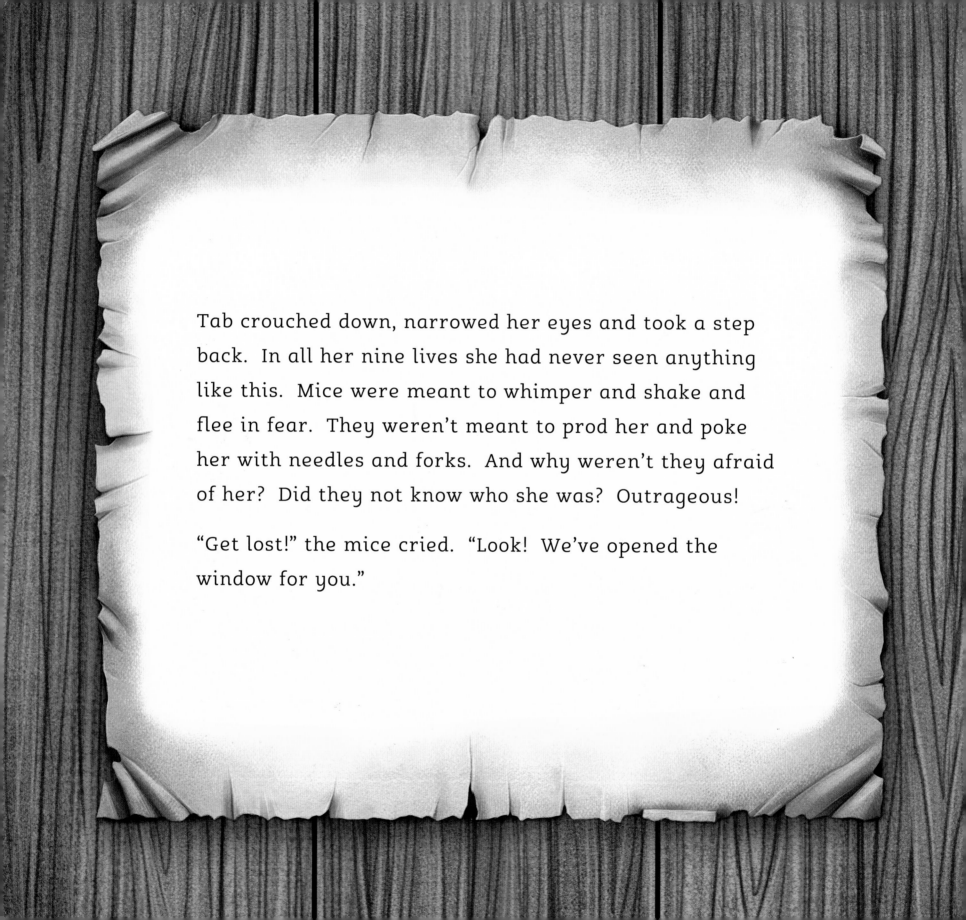

Tab crouched down, narrowed her eyes and took a step back. In all her nine lives she had never seen anything like this. Mice were meant to whimper and shake and flee in fear. They weren't meant to prod her and poke her with needles and forks. And why weren't they afraid of her? Did they not know who she was? Outrageous!

"Get lost!" the mice cried. "Look! We've opened the window for you."

Brave Gawain jumped onto Tab's head. "Tell all your cat friends about the mice of Raven Castle," he hissed. And with that he bit Terrible Tab on the ear.

"Meooooow!" Tab cried, and she leaped for the window with Gawain still hanging from her ear. As she sprang through the window, Gawain let go and Tab shot like an arrow into the dark night.

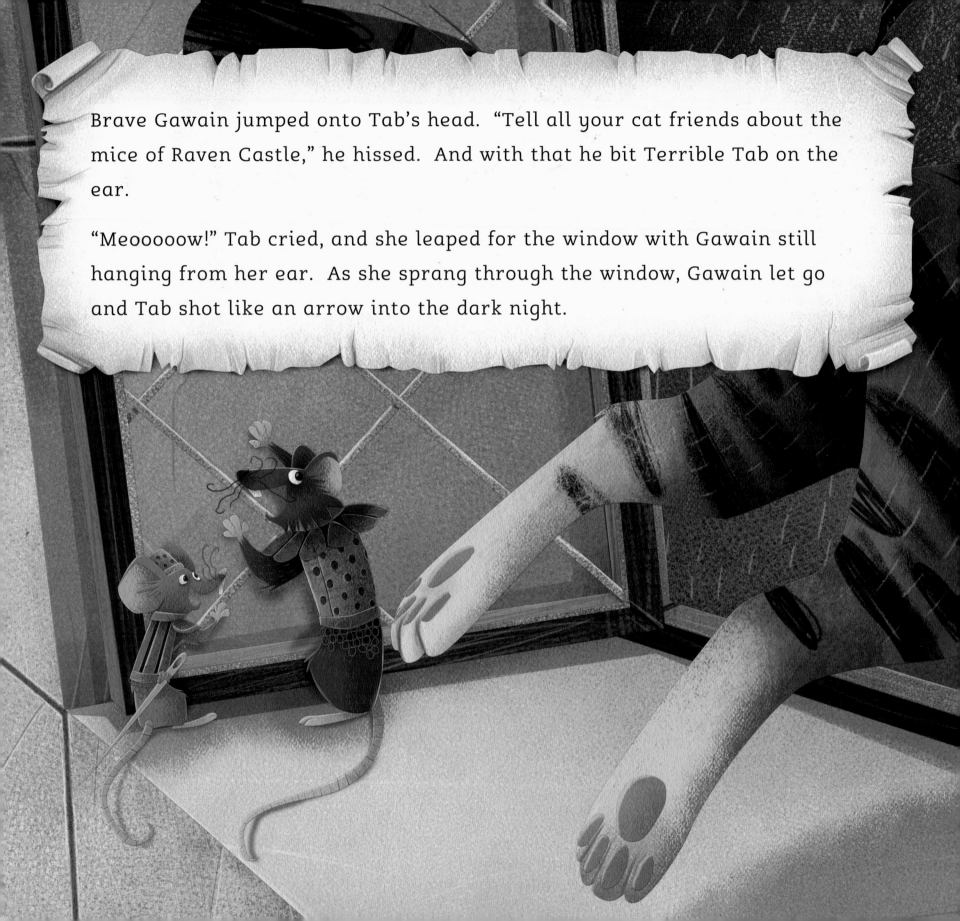

The four mice slammed the window shut as hard as they could.

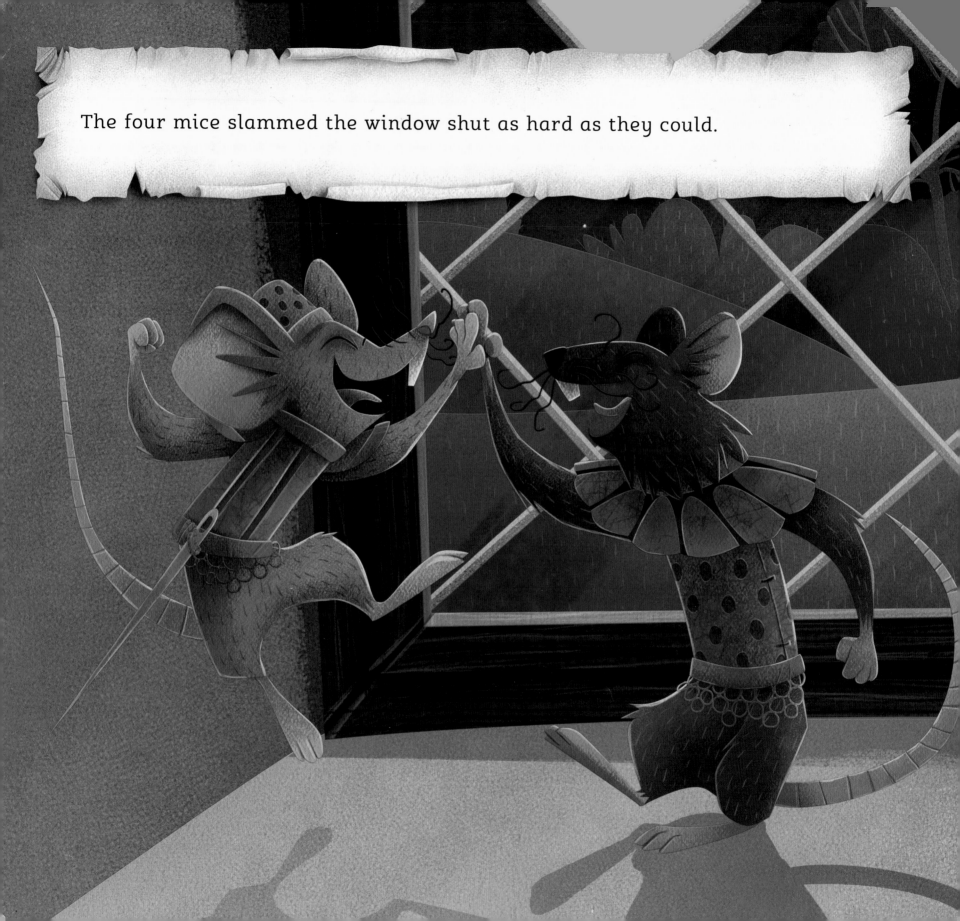

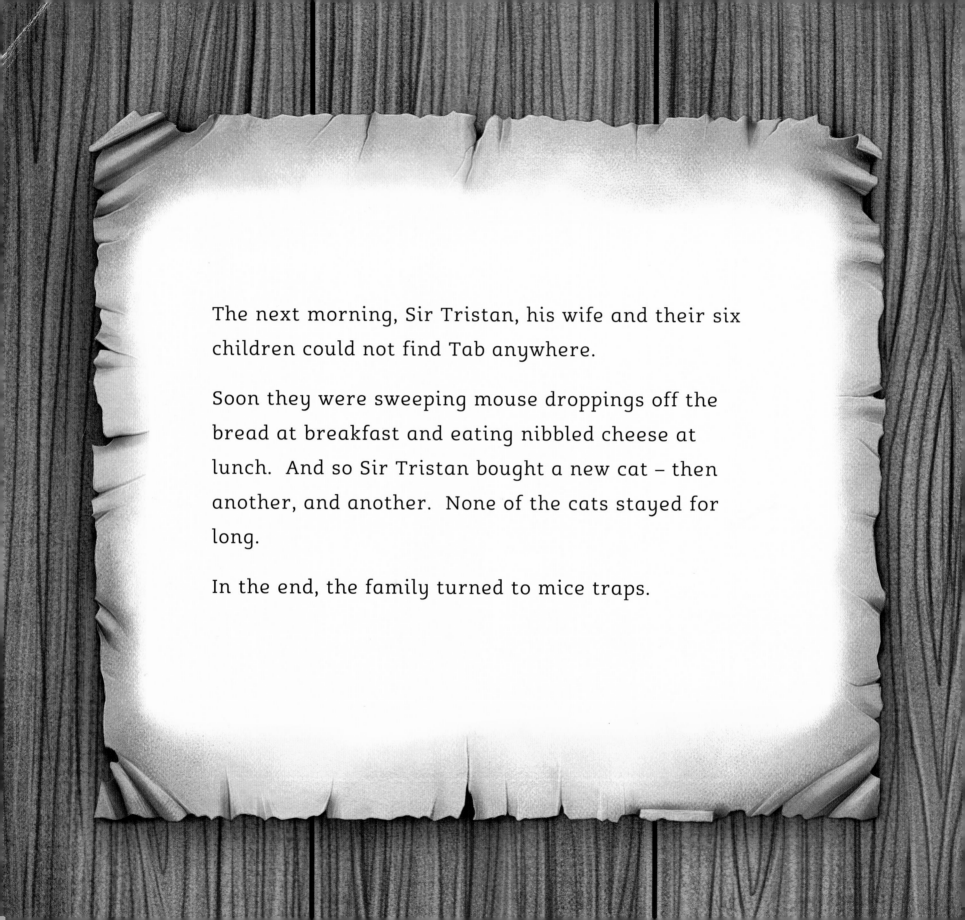

The next morning, Sir Tristan, his wife and their six children could not find Tab anywhere.

Soon they were sweeping mouse droppings off the bread at breakfast and eating nibbled cheese at lunch. And so Sir Tristan bought a new cat – then another, and another. None of the cats stayed for long.

In the end, the family turned to mice traps.

But all they ever found in them were forks and needles.

Grow a love of reading

PICTURE SQUIRRELS